SANTA MARIA PUBLIC LIBRARY

D0609565

Discarded by
Santa Maria Library

j 796.32309 W616

Anderson, Joan.
Rookie : Tamika Whitmore's
first year in the WNBA
c2000.

Orcutt Br.   NOV 19 2001

BRANCH COPY

GAYLORD MG

Rookie

TAMiKA WHiTMORE'S FiRST YEAR iN THE WNBA

TEXT BY
Joan Anderson

PHOTOGRAPHS BY
Michelle V. Agins

WITH A FOREWORD BY
Teresa Weatherspoon

Dutton Children's Books   New York

To Shelly, whose athletic prowess and support of women's sports
have been an enormous inspiration to me
—J.A.

To my family: Mom (Mrs. Price), Carol Lee, Caed, Kessie, and Alejandro.
And to my friends, Kelli Givens and Carol Rielly, who sat courtside at Liberty games and cheered me on!
—M.V.A.

ACKNOWLEDGMENTS

My gratitude to the WNBA, Liberty General Manager Carol Blazejowski, and Public Relations Director Maureen Coyle, for their help in making it possible to do this book. Being among disciplined and talented athletes was a tremendous privilege. My thanks to: Teresa Weatherspoon, for her time and thoughts; Joye Lee-McNelis, Tamika's college coach, for answering questions regarding Tamika's growth and development; and Gwen Glover, Tamika's mother, for all the early stories and rich memorabilia of her daughter's progress from high school to college. Her thoughts helped me flesh out the story of a determined athlete. Most of all, I am indebted to the rookie herself, Tamika Whitmore, who was most gracious in sharing her heart and soul about what it takes to become a professional women's basketball player. Finally, thanks to Cris Reeves and other fans who were willing to share their front-row seats with this visiting journalist. —J.A.

Special thanks to Carol Blazejowski, the General Manager of the New York Liberty, Maureen Coyle and Brad Topper, of the Liberty public relations department, and to Lisa White, the Liberty's ace trainer. Thanks to WNBA President Val Ackerman for her encouragement to do a book on the WNBA. Thanks also to Mark Pray, Gail Fuller, and Beth Marshall.
  Every photographer needs an angel, and Brandon Remiler of Fuji Film was mine. Thanks for lending me a few rolls of film for the project.
  And special thanks to the entire New York Liberty team for allowing me to be more than a beat sports photographer.
  With special thanks to Judge Karen Smith. —M.V.A.

Every effort has been made to trace the source of the visual material included in this book. The author and publisher regret any possible omissions and would welcome the inclusion of any missing credits in future printings of this title.

PAGE 7: photo of Tamika and Niesha courtesy of Sears, Tupelo. Photo of Tamika, Niesha, and Roxie Hughes courtesy of Johnny Addison. PAGE 9: photo and article, "Girls: Whitmore top player, Kemp coach," reprinted by permission of the *Northeast Mississippi Daily Journal*, Tupelo. PAGE 11: "Nothing 'Meek' about Whitmore in post at Memphis," copyright 1998, *USA Today*. Reprinted with permission. Accompanying photograph by Gil Michaels' Photography. Articles "One tough Tiger," with photo by Shoun A. Hill, copyright 1997, and "Lady Tigers top Bearcats," copyright 1998 by *The Commercial Appeal*, Memphis, Tennessee. Used with permission. PAGE 12: "Whitmore goes to N.Y. in the 3rd Round," with photo by Lance Murphey, copyright 1999 by *The Commercial Appeal*, Memphis, Tennessee. Used with permission.

Text copyright © 2000 by Joan Anderson
Photographs copyright © 2000 by Michelle V. Agins
Foreword copyright © 2000 by Teresa Weatherspoon • All rights reserved. • CIP Data is available.
Published in the United States by Dutton Children's Books, a division of Penguin Putnam Books for Young Readers
345 Hudson Street, New York, New York 10014 • www.penguinputnam.com
Designed by Ellen M. Lucaire • Printed in China • First Edition
1 2 3 4 5 6 7 8 9 10
ISBN 0-525-46412-3

Teresa Weatherspoon and Tamika Whitmore stretch before a big game.

Foreword

When I was a rookie I feared no one, but I respected the veterans who had paved the way. Rookies shouldn't be cocky, but they must be confident in their abilities and have a strong work ethic and willingness to learn. With these qualities, they will get respect from the other members of the team very fast. But, of course, it's also important for the more experienced players to offer a hand and advice.

Becky Hammon, another rookie on our team, told me that what she did in college meant nothing once she got to the WNBA. She had to prove herself all over again. All the young rookies on the Liberty—Becky Hammon, Michele VanGorp, and Tamika Whitmore—worked hard. As the season progressed, they felt like a part of the team. Being drafted isn't enough to make you a team member; it's your contribution and attitude that earns your place.

With Rebecca Lobo out for the season, Tamika was placed in a big role and she was never intimidated. Whether she played for two minutes or twenty, she believed in herself from the start and showed absolute effort. It's hard to prove your value in just two minutes of playing time, but Tamika's intensity showed immediately.

For a rookie or any other player, off-season is every bit as important as on-season. That's when you work on strengthening your weaknesses. After my first season, I worked on my shooting, playing games with guys who would be tough on me. I think it's also good to look at a lot of game film of yourself, to watch what you did well and what you didn't do so well. It's important to concentrate more on the not-so-well. You want everything about your game to be strong. Tamika says she's taking up boxing. That's wonderful. Her footwork and her stamina will improve. You use a lot of energy in just two minutes of boxing. Tamika will need the energy next season; we expect great things of her.

—TERESA WEATHERSPOON
Point Guard, New York Liberty

7t's a big day for Tamika Whitmore. If her team, the New York Liberty, beats the Washington Mystics tonight, they will clinch first place in their conference and a spot in the play-offs of the WNBA, the Women's National Basketball Association. Not many people expected the Liberty to do well this season. Ranked fourth at the beginning of the summer, they lost their star forward, Rebecca Lobo, to injury in their very first game. The Liberty have played hard for this chance. Teresa Weatherspoon's great defense and Crystal Robinson's sure shooting from the outside have helped them defeat many teams. But they haven't beaten Washington yet. The Liberty need strong playing on the inside, just in front of the basket, to pull this one off.

Tamika Whitmore, a six-foot, two-inch center for the Liberty, could make the difference. But she is a rookie, a new player. Her teammates and even her coach cannot be sure she'll do what's needed. There is just one person who is certain: Tamika. She has worked very hard to get here, too.

Vickie Johnson,
Tamika Whitmore,
and Kym Hampton

A solitary young woman with a serious expression of her face most of the time, Tamika has been on a mission since she was thirteen.

"My career really began the day I read a newspaper article about a girl in my hometown of Tupelo, Mississippi. She was getting a college scholarship to play basketball. That was enough motivation for me to learn to play, because there was no other way I could afford to go to college. When I told my mama, she must have thought I was crazy since I hadn't shown any interest in basketball up until then. My six-foot, seven-inch mama, a former high school player, became my first coach. She took me out to the backyard and taught me the basics.

Tamika, age three,
and her sister, Niesha,
age four

Tamika (in pink), age five,
and her sister (in blue),
age six, with their cousin,
Roxie Hughes

"Mama said, 'If you're serious, then you have to start playing with the boys because they will be tough on you.' I would ride my bike into town, get into a game, and play until dark. I was usually the last one picked for a team, but I didn't care, I just wanted to learn to play. When I wasn't in a pickup game, Mama would play defense for me so I could practice new shots I'd seen on my grandmother's television. And if no one was around to play with me, I'd set up an obstacle course with rocks and dribble around them as if they were opposing players.

"My mama's my hero," Tamika says. "Maya Angelou's poem 'Still I Rise' is all about my mama: *You may trod me in the very dirt / But still, like dust, I'll rise.* She's risen above so much, bringing up two daughters on seventy-five dollars a week as a housemaid. When I was very small, we lived in a house with no hot water, electricity, or a television. At night we used kerosene lamps. Mama made sure we had what we needed, though. When I look back on what Mama did, I realize that if you want something in life you have to work for it."

Tamika in high school

Tamika first played on a real team in middle school, but she sat on the bench a lot at first. "I didn't like the bench, so I would stay after-hours, practicing my shooting. When my cousin broke the high school scoring record with forty-five points in one game, I made up my mind to break it myself. The coach noticed my determination and gave me more playing time. By the end of the year I led the team in rebounds, assists, and points. I was ready for the high school team and a shot at my cousin's record!"

"Between ninth and tenth grade I had a growth spurt. This made me valuable to the high school coach, John McAdams. One of his star players had moved to another town, which left a spot open in the starting lineup. I was nervous that first game and got only ten points. But during the second game, I got twenty-seven. For the rest of school, I averaged twenty-eight points per game."

Tamika in her Mississippi All Stars uniform

Girls: Whitmore top player, Kemp coach

By BOBBY PEPPER
Daily Journal

Saltillo coach James Kemp admits his girls basketball team didn't have a consistent big scorer this year — someone like Tupelo's Tamika Whitmore.

While Whitmore's 21-point-per-game average carried the Lady Wave, Kemp's Lady Tigers were top scorers by committee. If a player scored 20 points in one game, another would score 20 the next.

"From one game to the next, we never knew who would be the top scorer," Kemp said.

Either way, Kemp's players and Whitmore got their points plus a few wins as both Tupelo (Class 5A) and Saltillo (Class 3A) advanced to the North Mississippi Tournament.

James Kemp

Kemp, who led Saltillo from a losing season to a North 3A berth, was selected by the Daily Journal sports staff as its Lee County Coach of the Year in girls basketball.

As for Whitmore, the 6-foot-1 junior who's already being courted by major colleges, she was picked the county's Player of the Year.

Kemp and Whitmore head the Daily Journal's first All-Lee County girls team, honoring the county's top players.

Saltillo's girls made the biggest turnaround of any county team, going from 8-22 in 1992-93 to 21-13 this season. With their balanced scoring — Saltillo's six regular players averaged between eight and 10 points a game — the Lady Tigers became the Division 1-3A runner-up.

"The most we've ever won in a season since I've been here is 12," said Kemp, who finished his 13th season at Saltillo. "I felt like we

Turn to GIRLS on back page

Her mother made sure that basketball did not get in the way of Tamika's schoolwork: "When a teacher called to inform me that Tamika had failed to hand in a term paper, I drove right over to the school and—to Tamika's horror—marched into the gym and told the coach that he would have to excuse her. We went home and she finished the paper that very night. After that, I never had another problem with Tamika and schoolwork."

But Tamika practiced basketball whenever she could, intent on improving her game. "Tamika knows what she wants," says Coach McAdams. By the end of her senior year, Tamika had met her twin goals: She beat her cousin's scoring record with forty-nine points in one game and had her pick of college scholarships.

Tamika was the most heavily recruited player Coach McAdams had ever seen. "The letters, as well as coaches, came pouring into Tupelo."

"Some called at two in the morning," Tamika remembers. "I couldn't stand the stress. I made a rule that anyone who called after ten P.M. was off my list."

She knew just what she wanted in a college program and had her own set of questions for the coaches: Did they have firm academic requirements and study hours? What kind of shoes and uniforms did they wear? (Tamika usually weighs between 185 and 200 pounds—she likes loose-fitting clothes.) How hard did they push their players? (Tamika likes to be pushed.) In the end, the University of Memphis volunteered all the right answers before Tamika got to ask the questions. "I said yes to Memphis before I even saw the place. After my decision, people joked that I was copying Elvis. He was born in Tupelo and ended up in Memphis."

Tamika had a reputation for intensity in college. Her teammates called her a gym rat because she spent up to four hours a day working out. She scored so many points in her four years at Memphis that she became the second-leading scorer in the history of the women's team. At games, fans shouted her nickname, Miko, and her number, 44. But Tamika felt the pressure at times; her favorite escape was writing poetry, which she still does to relax.

While Tamika was in college, a big change took place in sports. A women's professional basketball league was started. Now the girl who saw basketball as a way to get a college education had a chance to keep playing when school was over. Tamika and other top college players from around the country hoped to be drafted by the WNBA.

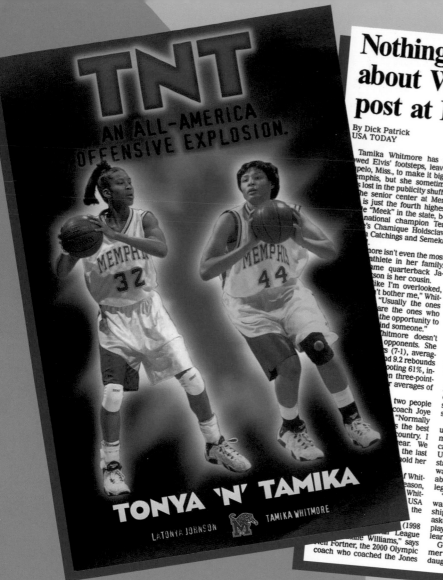

TNT
AN ALL-AMERICA OFFENSIVE EXPLOSION.

TONYA 'N' TAMIKA

LATONYA JOHNSON · TAMIKA WHITMORE

Nothing 'Meek' about Whitmore in post at Memphis

By Dick Patrick
USA TODAY

Jones Cup standout: Tamika Whitmore averaged 9.8 points and 6.2 rebounds a game, No. 2 on the U.S. team that won in Taiwan.

Tamika Whitmore has followed Elvis' footsteps, leaving Tupelo, Miss., to make it big in Memphis, but she sometimes is lost in the publicity shuffle. The senior center at Memphis is just the fourth highest-profile "Meek" in the state, behind national champion Tennessee's Chamique Holdsclaw, Tamika Catchings and Semeka [...]

Whitmore isn't even the most noted athlete in her family. Arena Football League quarterback Ja[...] Johnson is her cousin.

"I feel like I'm overlooked, but it doesn't bother me," Whitmore says. "Usually the ones who are the ones who have the opportunity to outscore someone."

But Whitmore doesn't mind her opponents. She [...] (7-1), averaging 9.2 rebounds [...] shooting 61%, including three-point [...] averages of [...]

There are two people [...] coach Joye [...] "Normally [...] the best [...] country. I [...] year. We [...] the last [...] hold her [...]

[...] of Whitmore's [...] season, [...] Whit[...] USA [...] the [...] (1998 [...] League [...] Williams," says [...] Neil Fortner, the 2000 Olympic coach who coached the Jones Cup team. "She may have more skills at this point because Natalie played (UCLA) volleyball.

"She's extremely versatile. She can play on the block; you can move her to the high post; she can shoot it from 15 (feet); she can put it on the floor."

Whitmore didn't take the usual path to the top. She didn't make the rounds of all-star camps and Amateur Athletic Union tournaments. She didn't start playing seriously until she was in ninth grade and read about a player earning a college scholarship.

"I told my mom that night I wanted a basketball scholarship," Whitmore said. "She asked me did I know how to play. I told her no, but I could learn. It went on from there."

Gwen Glover, 6-7 and a former prep player, took her daughter to a backyard court to demonstrate the basics.

"If there was a move I saw on TV, I'd say, 'Mom, you've got to let me try this on you,' " Whitmore says. "I figured if I could do a move on her, I could do it on anybody."

Glover taught more than post moves. Before remarrying when Whitmore was about 7, she raised two daughters by herself, earning as little as $75 a week as a domestic.

For about five years, the family lived in a shack without electricity and warm water.

"It wasn't like I didn't get what I wanted," Whitmore says. "I never asked for much. The thing I asked for most was fruit rollups.

"I made it a goal that when I became of age, I wanted to be there for my mom like she was there for me and my sister."

Whitmore's a hot pro prospect now. She arrived at Memphis in 1995 with lots of potential and extra weight at 210 pounds. "I had dimples on my elbows," the 185-pounder says.

She did extra running and became a gym rat, often returning to the gym at night with guys after practice. She absorbed the finer points of post play from the coaching staff.

When not in the gym, she's often in her room, studying, writing poetry or watching instructional videos or old movies.

"My mother always told me if I want something, go get it," Whitmore says. "That's what I've been doing."

My Tree

Sometimes, I just need to get away,
Away from those problems that nag day to day.
I need, no, want to be free, so to be free,
I go, disappear, and climb high in my tree.
Tucked far in the woods of my mind,
No one can find me standing still in time.
Listening to the breeze,
Rustling through the dead leaves.
I escape the world, so I can feel free
From all the problems that bother me.
I escape, escape from me,
When I go and climb my tree.
Miko #44

U of M's Whitmore keys team win streak

By Phil Stukenborg
The Commercial Appeal

The revelation came instantly for University of Memphis women's basketball player Tamika Whitmore, about as quick as one of her spin moves to the basket.

As a freshman at Tupelo (Miss.) High, Whitmore had watched her cousin, Sonia White, emerge as a standout basketball player, earning all-state honors and a scholarship to Austin Peay.

"I got to thinking," Whitmore said. "I said I've got [...] more years of school left [...] I'm going to do what she did. [...] decided to take up basketball [...] I told my mom that I was [...] ing to play, get a scholar[...] and go to college."

[...] hen the Lady Tigers play [...] Southern Mississippi in a [...] ference USA game Friday [...] at Hattiesburg, Miss., [...] will be led by a 6-2 sopho[...] center who followed [...] on her promise.

[...] a very headstrong per[...] Whitmore said. "When I [...] mind to do something, [...] ng to do it. I don't care [...] in the way."

Gwendolyn Glover, [...] e's mother, had no [...] her daughter would [...] Whitmore began [...] a 10th grader, aver[...] points and 16.8 re[...] the time she was a [...] accepted a scholar[...] from the U of M.

[...] onths into her soph[...] son, Whitmore has [...] ey component of a

ONE TOUGH TIGER

University of Memphis sophomore center Tamika Whitmore battles for a rebound during the Lady Tigers' game [...] Charlotte on Jan. 17. With Whitmore leading the way, the Lady Tigers have won seven straight games.

team that is 15-4, has won seven straight, is 7-1 in C-USA and on the verge of a national ranking.

Whitmore is averaging a team-leading 19.4 points and 8 rebounds and is shooting 62.8 percent from the field, which ranks sixth nationally. She has led the Lady Tigers in scoring in 11 of the past 14 games and in rebounding 10 times during the same stretch.

Not surprisingly, the Lady Tigers are 12-2 during that period, which began with the team's 96-74 win over Mississippi State Dec. 13. The only two losses came to Louisville (7-0 in C-USA) and then-No. 22 LSU.

Whitmore's contributions have come while several veteran players have, at various times, struggled.

"She has put us on her back and carried us," said Lady Tiger coach Joye Lee-McNelis. "She is just going and getting every bucket we need. She is p[...] hunger."

Glover, who st[...] played no small [...] more's developm[...] former high scho[...] in Tupelo, taught [...] ter the game's fir[...]

Please see TIGER[...]

Lady Tigers top Bearcats

Second-half surge lifts U of M into C-USA title game

By Phil Stukenborg
The Commercial Appeal

LOUISVILLE, Ky. — As the University of Memphis women's basketball team entered its locker room at Louisville Gardens during halftime of Sunday's Conference USA Tournament semifinal game against Cincinnati, Lady Tiger coach Joye Lee-McNelis was already busy scribbling on the blackboard.

Her message was brief, only four letters, but it made an impression. On the board she wrote: N-C-A-A.

If her Lady Tigers were to make their fourth straight NCAA Tournament appearance, Lee-McNelis informed them they would have to play the final 20 minutes differently than they did the previous 20.

What they did in the second half was shoot 59.1 percent, hold Cincinnati to 34.1 percent and outrebound the Bearcats, 19-11, in a 72-64 win.

Memphis (21-7) advanced to tonight's 6:30 (CST) championship game against the school's biggest rival, Louisville. The Lady Cardinals beat Marquette, 77-66, in the second semifinal.

"What a game, what a game," Lee-McNelis said. "I felt if we could keep it up-tempo, we could pull it out."

The U of M trailed at the half, 30-25, and appeared in danger of being bounced from the semifinals for the second straight year. But Lee-McNelis preached fear and her team listened.

Actually, they heeded the warning in the first five minutes of the half. A 9-0 run gave the Lady Tigers a 34-30 lead, an advantage that eventually reached 12 before the U of M settled for its eight-point win.

"Our players stepped up and exerted defensive intensity in the first five minutes of the second half," Lee-McNelis said.

The Lady Tigers began their second-half run 12 seconds into the half. Point guard Yolanda Reed buried a three-pointer from the left corner. Then Tamika Whitmore dropped in a 14-footer and Reed followed her own missed three-point attempt with a short jumper.

"We went in the locker room and we knew [...]

Please see U OF M, Page D3

C-USA Tournament		
(at Louisville, Ky.)		
SUNDAY		
■ (1) Memphis 72, (5) Cincinnati 64		
■ (2) Louisville 77, (3) Marquette 66		
TODAY		
■ 6:30 p.m. CST — (1) Memphis vs. (2) Louisville; ESPN2 (delayed, 10:30 p.m.)		

Lady Tiger center Tamika Whitmore shoots through the defense of Cincinnati's Jewel Snowden (left) and Amber Stocks during the U of M semifinal victory.

11

Whitmore goes to N.Y. in 3rd round

By Phil Stukenborg
The Commercial Appeal

During University of Memphis women's basketball player Tamika Whitmore's stellar career, she was an intimidator. Rarely was she intimidated.

Until Tuesday.

Whitmore, the second-leading scorer in U of M history, was so nervous Tuesday morning awaiting her selection in the WNBA Draft that she couldn't take her scheduled sociology exam. "My teacher told me to come back tomorrow," she said.

So Whitmore walked over the U of M athletic office building, sat in coach Joye Lee-McNelis's office and listened to the draft on the Internet along with her mother, Gwen Glover,

her stepfather, Glenn Glover, Lee-McNelis and the U of M assistant coaches.

Then midway through the third round of the four-round draft, Whitmore was chosen by the New York Liberty. She was the 30th player taken and one of only 11 college players selected. Players from the dissolved American Basketball League dominated the draft selections.

With New York, Whitmore will join one of the league's marquee players, Rebecca Lobo, in the nation's top media market.

"Broadway better look out," Lee-McNelis said, referring to her outspoken post player. "New York will never be the same."

Whitmore, the seventh college player chosen in the draft,

was expecting Detroit, with the 29th pick overall, to take her. Coach Nancy Lieberman-Cline had been impressed with Whitmore's pre-draft camp performance in Chicago and had closely followed her career.

But Detroit opted for Alabama's Dominique Canty and New York, coached by former Dallas Mavericks coach Richie Adubato, chose Whitmore, who led the nation in scoring (26.3 ppg) as a senior. Whitmore was the sixth pick in the third round.

"I thought she would go higher after talking to different scouts," Lee-McNelis said. "I know they thought she'd be among the top five college players taken. But you have to look at team's needs, too."

Whitmore, a Tupelo, Miss., native, said she was disappoin-

By Lance Murphey

Tamika Whitmore (center) waits with her mother, Gwen Glover (left) and Tiger coach Joye-Lee McNelis during Tuesday's WNBA draft. Whitmore was selected by the New York Liberty.

ted by her draft position. "I just would have liked to have been appreciated a little more," she said. "I guess I'll have to go prove myself

again."

Training camp opens for WNBA teams May 14 and the

Please see **TAMIKA**, Page **D6**

"We watched the WNBA draft on TV," Tamika remembers. "I was sitting in my coach's office at the University of Memphis with my mother and stepfather, anxious about who was going to take me. In college basketball, you pick the school you play for. In professional basketball, you have no idea what team you'll be on or even where you will live until the moment your name is called. The draft had reached the third round, but no team had picked me yet. I was disappointed.

"There were rumors that I would go to Detroit, but this round they picked Dominique Canty [a player from the University of Alabama]. The very next pick was by the New York Liberty. My name appeared on the screen and I was stunned. I hadn't really thought about New York. But I didn't actually care where I went as long as I got some playing time. Usually rookies spend a lot of time on the bench.

"It was a happy and sad week for me. My grandpa died that Friday, we buried him on Saturday, and I flew to New York late that night, arriving at 1 A.M. on Sunday. Later that morning, I reported to the Reebok Gym [where the Liberty train] for a scrimmage, and the very first person I met was Teresa Weatherspoon. There I was, dressed in cutoffs and a jersey, introducing myself to this great player. 'I already know who you are,' T-Spoon said. 'You got an accent on you.'"

"I didn't try to fit in—I just had it in my head to play well right from the start. At the end of that scrimmage, T-Spoon said: 'Girl, you can play.'"

After the first few games of the year, the team held an open practice for season ticket holders. Tamika was introduced to the crowd by her teammates as the rookie of the year because she had played so hard and showed she wasn't afraid to take the ball to the hoop.

Michelle VanGorp, Tamika, Venus Lacy, and Coquese Washington

*Coquese and Tamika
wait to board a plane*

"Being a rookie in the pros," says Tamika, "means starting out again at another level, in a different environment, with a lot of uncertainty and unexpected things coming at you every single day."

"First, living in New York is a big adjustment," she says. "I wasn't ready for the noise, going to sleep listening to car horns instead of crickets. I had to learn how to hail a cab—we don't have taxis in Tupelo!—keep track of my expenses, and live in a hotel with the rest of the team. And traveling on airplanes to away games is awful. I hate flying. I figure if we were meant to fly, God would have given us wings. I also don't like to be out of touch with my family for long, so I have a cell phone with me wherever I go. I call my mom almost every day."

This morning she is sleeping in after a grueling road trip to Utah, Arizona, and Texas, nestled with a teddy bear that some fan gave her during a game. "I thought it was kind of cute," she says, insisting that it's not a lucky mascot. "I don't believe in luck," she continues. "Things happen for a reason. You always have to be ready to deal with the good and the bad."

On a non-game day, she would be up early and out to the gym, where the Liberty's trainer, Lisa White, has set up a personal routine of weight training and conditioning for each member of the team. "We work on different parts of the body on specific days," Tamika says. "Mondays I lift weights to strengthen my upper body; Tuesdays I work my legs, lower back, and abdomen; Wednesdays the focus is on my back, shoulders, and abdomen; and Fridays I do a total body workout."

Her precious sleep time is interrupted by a knock on the door.

In walks Teresa Weatherspoon, the point guard of the Liberty. Point guards guide the team on the court, but Spoon is an off-court leader, too, making sure her teammates feel psyched up and ready for games. She is carrying a tape of a television interview with Tamika. T-Spoon pops it into the VCR and pokes fun at the segment while tossing a basketball to the laughing Tamika.

"I have a special relationship with Spoon," Tamika says. "Living in the same hotel has made it easy for us to hang out. We watch a lot of game film, and Spoon gives me pointers on how to improve. She's my mentor. I've learned so much from her, not just about basketball but about being a person."

Teresa Weatherspoon and Tamika

Spoon is even more intense than usual; tonight's game is important. "There's no way we're losing," she says as she twirls the ball on her fingertip.

"I'm right there with you," says Tamika, hopping up and nearly tripping over her size 14 shoes. Tamika sends the ball back to Spoon as an impromptu pickup game ensues. The hotel furniture is spared, though, when the two start dancing to a CD by the group Naughty By Nature, a Liberty favorite. "You can't help but be pulled in by Spoon," Tamika says. "Kym Hampton [another Liberty veteran] says that if Spoon can't get you pepped up, you're probably dead."

Eventually Spoon leaves, and Tamika begins her pregame rituals. She has an early lunch, high in carbohydrates, at a nearby diner. Her favorite waitress greets her with "Here's my girl!" and asks for an autograph for a young relative.

After lunch, Tamika heads right back to her hotel room. She is feeling sluggish, so she takes an ice bath, hopping gingerly into a tub of ice cubes. "It's a shock to your body when you first get in," she says. "It numbs you completely, but it gets your blood circulating. Not only do I feel refreshed, I feel like I have a brand-new pair of arms and legs."

She then soaks her feet in warm water and rubs away any rough skin with a pumice stone. "I pride myself in never having a blister," she says. With all the running she does on court, a blister could be a serious distraction. "I keep my feet in good shape. Off the court I wear flip-flops or sandals."

Just before leaving for Madison Square Garden, the big arena where the Liberty play, Tamika calls her mom. "We talk shop and cover the emotional stuff," her mother says. "I always want to make sure she's eating well and I ask how the coach is treating her. I try to read between the lines and pick up any problems she might be having."

Feeling calm and with her game face firmly in place, Tamika heads out to hail a taxi to the Garden.

In the cab, she studies her book of basketball plays and thinks about some of the typical moves of the opposing players. In tonight's game her goals are clear. "I want to play my usual role, to give the starting players, Kym [Hampton] and Sue [Wicks], a rest when they need it . . . be productive, provide a spark . . . blessed be that I will be able to do it all."

Tamika makes her way into the Garden. She flashes her ID to a security guard and walks through a maze of underground tunnels until she reaches the locker room. She's the first player to arrive. "I like to get to the locker room three hours before game time," Tamika says. "There's a lot to do, but more than anything I just want to be in a basketball environment."

Other players arrive, and soon the locker room is bustling with intensity, filling up now with the press (who have access before and after the game), plus trainers, coaches, the Liberty public relations staff, and an occasional family member or friend.

The Liberty players are like family themselves. "These are the only people I see for three months," Tamika says. "We work out, practice, and, when we're on the road, share rooms and meals. It feels like summer camp. We have a lot of sisterhood going on, especially tonight up against Washington. Losing to them three times has made our camaraderie even stronger.

"I'm especially close to Kym," Tamika says. "She looks like my mom and calls me her little sister."

But now, hours before the game, players go into their own solitary space for a while, oblivious of the chaos around them. Some read a magazine or book, stretch, watch videos of their opponents' recent games, or gather around Coach Richie Adubato as he highlights strategies for tonight. They need time to think about their own roles in the game before they are ready to get psyched up as a team.

Tamika has a lot to consider. "During games, I see moves I've never seen before," she explains. "And I am not watching the whole game from the bench, as rookies often do. With Rebecca [Lobo] out, I have been playing an average of twenty minutes a game, so I have to learn *as I play!*"

*Tamika with Coach
Richie Adubato*

She grabs a couple of pieces of gum, settles next to her locker, puts on her ear phones, and meditates to gospel music for ninety minutes. "If you keep God first, everything will turn out for the best," she says. "I pray for each member of the team and then visualize how the game could go."

Then it's off to the trainer to have her ankle taped up, a lingering memory of the one bad day she's had all season. "I got undercut from behind in the Phoenix game and sprained my ankle," she recalls. "It kept me out of four games in three weeks. Up until then I had never missed a game or practice due to injury, even in college or high school. It was hard sitting out of games, feeling as though the team was growing without me. I am playing through some pain now."

Trainer Lisa White
with Tamika

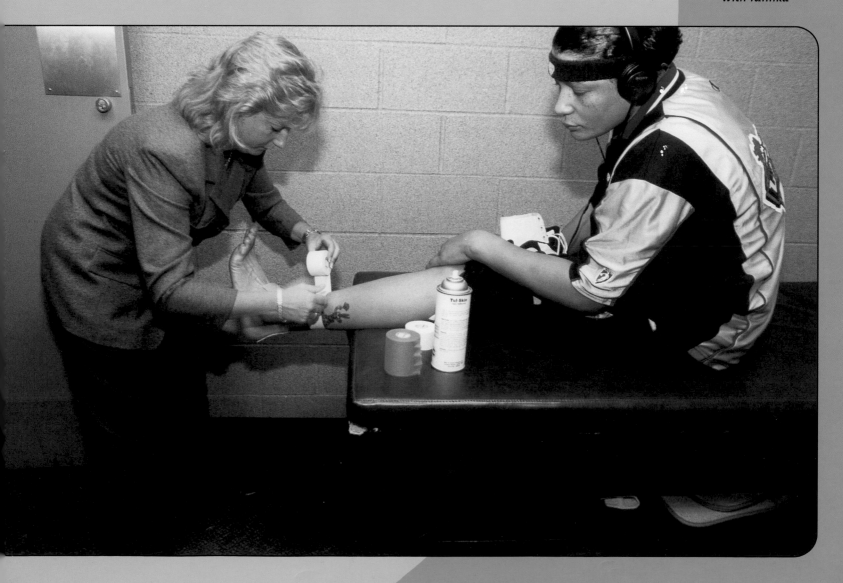

Sue Wicks and Tamika head out for warm-up.

It's an hour before game time. Tamika and her teammates head out on the court for warm-up. They take layups, foul shots, and give-and-goes. "I want to keep my hands loose," Tamika says, "work up a sweat, talk to the fans, and have a little fun."

Sue Wicks limbers up her feet with hops and skips across the court. Tamika and T-Spoon chat as they stretch. Crystal Robinson, a forward, shoots endlessly from the three-point mark. Then Tamika takes her turn at the hoop, starting in close and gradually working her way out. Tonight every practice shot except one goes in the basket.

Dressed in Liberty shirts and green Statue of Liberty crowns, young fans pour through the turnstiles and are greeted by the Liberty mascot, Maddie, who gets the crowd cheering. There is a circuslike atmosphere inside the big dome of Madison Square Garden. The Liberty Torch Patrol, a group of dancers and cheerleaders, rehearses in center court while television and press crews stake out their courtside space.

Commentators like Hall of Famer Ann Meyers test their microphones and sign autographs as ball girls place plenty of Gatorade, towels, and basketballs within easy reach of the players.

Maddie, the Liberty mascot

Liberty fans!

The New York Liberty are pumped up. It helps to be at home for such a crucial game. "We have the momentum of the crowd behind us," says Tamika, "which always fires the starting lineup." Just before the game, a group of ten-year-olds from New Jersey comes out on the court. This local team has been invited by the Liberty to participate in the ball toss, a tradition in which Liberty players present each girl with a brand-new basketball to keep. The ball is followed by a big hug. Because of the WNBA, these girls have a chance to become professional athletes someday, and the Liberty players want to encourage them to keep playing the game.

Sophia Witherspoon, Coquese, Kym, and Tamika give encouraging hugs to young players.

Vickie Johnson, Coquese Washington, Becky Hammon, Sophia Witherspoon, Tamika Whitmore, Kym Hampton, Rebecca Lobo (obscured), Michele VanGorp (obscured), Sue Wicks, Teresa Weatherspoon, Venus Lacy, and Maddie: the Liberty!

As the mostly female crowd of over 15,000 cheer, Kym Hampton walks to center court and belts out her rendition of the national anthem while her teammates sway to the sounds.

Any apprehension about beating Washington has been worked through. "Tonight we're playing for each other," says Tamika. "It's Kym's last season and Spoon has been trying for so long. We've vowed that we're not going to lose."

Coach Adubato gathers the team and says: "You all understand what needs to be done. Now go do it!" The starting lineup heads for the court. Tamika and her other teammates will watch and wait from the bench.

It's time for the tip-off. Vickie Johnson gets the ball, dribbles it downcourt, and makes a basket within the first few seconds. The crowd roars and waves their handmade signs with messages like YOU GO, GIRL! and GIVE ME LIBERTY OR GIVE ME DEATH!

Vickie gets a shot past Monica Maxwell.

Kym and Crystal do not want Shalonda Enis to have the ball.

Coquese gets a hug from Spoon.

Spurred on by Kym Hampton's eighteen-foot shot and several three-pointers by Crystal Robinson, the Liberty runs out to a 15–4 lead and doesn't look back. Every good move by a Liberty player is rewarded by bear hugs, butt pats, and high fives from T-Spoon. Her own playing is fierce; she makes the expression "in your face" a reality as she blocks and stops the Mystic stars Nikki McCray and Chamique Holdsclaw. All the while, the Garden's organ pumps out music to stir the fans. They willingly chant DE-FENSE! DE-FENSE! each time Washington gets possession of the ball.

On the bench, Tamika can barely sit still. She shouts to the players on the court, discusses every big move with her teammates on the bench, and waits to get into the game.

Becky, Rebecca, Tamika, Michele, Sophia, and Venus

"When I cross over the line, I try to do something positive right away," Tamika says. "My head is full of thoughts—things like, what is the other defense up to, what do I need to offer to counter them, where is each player going with the ball, where do they each shoot from best?" Her poker face has caused people to label her as mean. Actually she is just focused and has little time to smile. "Some people say I'm intimidating," she says, sounding defensive. "My mentality is—there's a ball to get, so I go get it.

"When I first have possession of the ball, I keep it under my chin, with elbows out. This allows me to make room to maneuver, gives me more space to work with as I move toward the hoop."

It doesn't take long for the coach to send Tamika into the game. "In Tamika," he has said, "I have a complete player. She's strong inside, has good balance, is a great rebounder, and she's fearless."

She shimmies into a throng of players, ball in hand, goes for the shot, and gets fouled. So Tamika makes her first trip of the night to the free-throw line. She drops two shots in the basket. By the end of the game, she'll have scored ten points from the foul line.

In the second half, the ferocious tempo of the game continues. Coach Adubato calls time out just to give the players a short break. The team, all breathing heavily, huddles around their coach as he shouts encouragement above the roar of the crowd. "Keep getting the ball inside. . . . C'mon now, don't let down. Get back in there and hit the bucket." But he gestures for Tamika to sit on the bench, sending Kym Hampton back in.

"I know it's my job to give Kym and Sue a rest," Tamika says, "but even so, I've always hated being taken out of the game once I'm in. When I am stuck on the bench, I see things that could have or should have been done and I go crazy. Rebecca [Lobo] says, 'Calm down, little rookie,' when I groan over a bad play."

Coach Adubato gives advice.

Tamika has the hot hand tonight, so she doesn't stay on the bench for long. She is improving with each game. Her college coach, Joye Lee-McNelis, says, "High-powered competition challenges her. She wants to excel. I picked her because she could run the floor, catch, and she has a sure touch. And she's gotten better playing with the WNBA veterans."

There is just one minute left on the clock. Tamika shoots again.

Not only is Tamika making her shots, but her strong defense is keeping the Mystics from getting baskets. Washington's Chamique Holdsclaw, the number-one draft pick of the season, is feeling Tamika's presence. A little rookie-versus-rookie competition is evident. "Tamika Whitmore is revitalizing the old legs of the Liberty," says one television commentator. "Nothing is stopping this rookie tonight."

Tamika blocks Chamique Holdsclaw as Kym guards Murriel Page.

Tamika and Spoon do the bump.

The buzzer sounds. The game is over. The fans shriek. The LIberty has won, 66-54. Tamika and Spoon rush together for a chest bump. Then they join their teammates for a midcourt victory huddle. Hands in the air tepee fashion, they give silent thanks for pulling it off. The team nobody had faith in during the pre-season has clinched a spot in the play-offs.

The Liberty huddle

Tamika scored twenty points, her highest total so far, and is named Player of the Game for the third time this season.

"How does it feel?" a journalist asks her at the postgame press conference.

"I was focused out there," she replies quietly but with a rare, big smile. "It feels good to clinch the play-off spot, but we've still got unfinished business. You can't ever be satisfied, because then you sit back and everything dwindles. We're halfway there. We need to take the remaining two games and work on our precision."

Coach Adubato is proud. "We played hard and Tamika was strong inside. With a rookie, you never know what she's going to give you. Tamika has proved powerful in the post."

Spoon shares her thoughts on the game.

Meanwhile the players relax in front of their lockers, looking relieved, tired, and gratified to be talking about victory.

"We were light on our feet," says guard Sophia Witherspoon.

"All of us had heart tonight," says Crystal Robinson. "Every game now is to get us into the championship."

"We had to win this one," says Spoon. "Praise God we got it tonight. Y'know, they tried to say the entire Eastern Conference was mediocre. Me, I say we have a winning mind-set. Call us arrogant or cocky, so be it. This game shows who we are and who we can be."

Tamika talks to the press.

Tamika is surrounded by reporters. She patiently answers every last question. Then, after a shower and change into fresh clothes, she heads out of the Garden to board a bus for the airport. There isn't time to rest or celebrate. The Liberty have an away game, the last of the season, in Cleveland. But happy satisfaction shows on Tamika's face. She has played her game and proved that she can be counted on.

A new home, a midseason injury, some bench-sitting, and big expectations—this rookie season hasn't been easy, but Tamika Whitmore is a determined woman. She is proof that you don't have to be picked first—on the playground, from the draft, or off the bench—to finish on top!

Laundry piles up.

After the victory against Charlotte, Vickie looks on as Tamika comforts an over-wrought Spoon.

The Postseason

The Liberty beat Charlotte in the play-offs, clinching their spot in the championship finals against Houston.

Liberty lost the first game at home, won game two in Houston with an amazing three-point desperation shot by Teresa Weatherspoon, but lost the third and deciding game. It wasn't Liberty's year. Even so, coming from fourth place to first is something to be celebrated. Plus, as Tamika says, "We added a blemish to Houston's perfect home-court record. We earned their respect.

"Ending such a great season on a loss was sad," says Tamika, "but even harder is leaving the team. It is like leaving family. They taught me so much. Women like Spoon and Kym, they helped me grow and improve."

Tamika meets
Venus Williams.

Tamika after
meeting Venus
Williams

Tamika, the new professional, spent her final days in New York at the U.S. Open Tennis Tournament. Not only did she get Venus Williams's autograph—a big thrill—but the tennis fans wanted hers as well.

She is heading back home to Mississippi. She will spend the off-season working at basketball camps for young girls, writing poetry, and driving around in her newly purchased pickup truck. She also plans to take up boxing, which should improve her defensive moves, increase her foot speed, and make her stronger and more agile. "I like playing in the post [in front of the basket]," she says, "but I'm looking to score more. Next season you'll see a much slimmer and fit Tamika. I aim to outrun everybody. I'll be stronger and bring problems to the defense on the opposing teams." She's a girl with game, and she aims to keep it that way.

Tamika
and a fan

Tamika Whitmore

TOTALS		AVERAGES PER GAME	
Games	27	Minutes	21.2
Points	214	Points	7.9
Field goals made/attempted	80/184	Field goals	3.0
Field goal percentage	.435		
3-pointers made/attempted	1/8	3-pointers	0.0
3-pointer percentage	.125		
Free throws made/attempted	53/78	Free throws	2.0
Free throw percentage	.679		
Rebounds	96	Rebounds	3.6
Assists	18	Assists	.7
Steals	16	Steals	.6
Blocks	6	Blocks	.2
Fouls	78	Fouls	2.9

GLOSSARY

assist *a pass that results in a score*

bucket *another name for the hoop or basket*

center *position usually played by the tallest member of a team. A center plays close to the basket, shooting, blocking opponent's shots, and trying to get rebounds.*

desperation shot *a game-ending shot, usually taken from half court with little or no chance of making the point*

draft *a lottery of top college or other players from which various teams choose their lineup*

forward *a position for taller players. Forwards usually play from the corners of the court to the foul lane. There are two forwards on a team.*

foul shots *also called free throws. These are awarded to a player when an opposing team member fouls her. Others aren't allowed to interfere with the shot. One point is earned for each basket.*

free-throw line *also called the foul line. This is where the player taking the foul shot stands.*

give-and-go *a play in which an offensive player passes the ball to a teammate and cuts toward the basket, expecting a return pass*

guard *a position for the smallest and quickest players. It requires good ball handling and defensive playing.*

hoop *another name for the basket*

hot hand *refers to the player who is handling the ball well and making most of her shots*

lane *the area, usually painted, in front of each basket and below the free-throw line*

layup *a one-handed jump shot from one side of the basket, usually banked off the backboard*

man-to-man *a type of defense in which a player has a specific opponent to defend*

point guard *the guard who handles the ball most and directs the offense*

the post *the area outside the lane but near the basket*

press *short for pressure, which refers to keeping defensive pressure on offensive players*

rebound *a missed shot that is retrieved by an attacker or defender*

rookie *a player in her first season*

scrimmage *a game played before the regular season that won't be part of the team's standings*

tip-off *the jump ball at the start of the game; a ball is thrown in the air and a player from each team jumps up and attempts to knock it to a teammate*